Our Daughter and Other Stories

by Wendy Oleson

Winner of the 2017 Rachel Wetzsteon Chapbook Prize

The Rachel Wetzsteon Chapbook Prize, awarded annually by the editors of *Map Literary*, honors the memory of our esteemed colleague—poet, editor, and professor at William Paterson University. The award rotates to include poetry, fiction, and nonfiction. This year's award was judged by Martha Witt and N. West Moss.

Map Literary is dedicated to celebrating quality works of new literature. Rather than aligning with any one aesthetic, we aspire to promote the finest provocative writing of our time, publishing semi-annual issues of original fiction, poetry, nonfiction and art in on online format, with yearly print anthologies of select work.

EDITOR
John Parras

The William Paterson University of New Jersey
College of Humanities and Social Sciences
Department of English
300 Pompton Road
Wayne, NJ 07470

www.wpunj.edu/mapliterary   mapliterary@wpunj.edu

Table of Contents

for Ann Boultinghouse

Acknowledgements

Enormous thanks to the editors who first published these selections: Tara Laskowski at *SmokeLong Quarterly* ("How I Liked the Avocados"); Jessica Alexander at *Quarterly West* ("Story of a Room"); Marco Kaye, Chris Normandin, and contest judge Karen Russell at *Washington Square Review* ("Bodies of Water"); Meg Pokrass at *New Flash Fiction Review* ("Our Daughter"); Joanna Luloff and Ian Stansel at *Memorious: A Journal of New Verse and Fiction* ("The Glass Girl"); Brian Mihok and Edward Mullany at *matchbook* ("Pin: A Fairy Tale"); Gordon Krupsky at *The MacGuffin* ("We Used to Play at Kmart"); Robert Long Foreman at *The Cossack Review* ("Record from a Farmhouse"); as well as Barbara Westwood Diehl at *Baltimore Review* and Robert James Russell at *Midwestern Gothic* ("Man Skate").

Our Daughter and Other Stories

HOW I LIKED THE AVOCADOS

I stuffed one in a knee-high boot, another in my make-up case, and nested the third in a cowl-neck sweater, an itchy Christmas gift from Greg's parents. I thought security would take your avocados (my avocados) if I didn't hide them deep in the suitcase. I'd heard rules about produce and quarantines; maybe I had a guilty conscience. I said I'd see you again before we left, but I couldn't get away.

Avocado #1:

Ripe before the other two, this is a mystery. Did it cook in my shoe under the plane? I called you in the bathroom on the layover and apologized to your voicemail. I still don't have any messages. When we get home I can't sleep; I eat the avocado in the dark, standing over the wooden cutting board. I eat the skin because it is thin and from your tree.

Avocado #2:

I take it from my sock drawer and open it before it's ready. I'm greedy. I'm wasteful. Careless. You won't call me back. In the other room, Greg watches television. The fruit is hard and yellow around the pit. It sinks in my stomach, and I have to throw some away, concealed in a paper towel, buried under three days of garbage, buried. When I return to the couch, he puts his feet on my lap, then lifts them away, confused. Honey? Weren't you going to get us a snack?

I have green flesh under my fingernails.

Avocado #3:

Greg comes home early. How strange, he says—he doesn't remember buying that avocado, but there it is, splayed across our cutting board. We eat it standing up. He gets out the salt and tells me about a new account: the account is good. Or is the avocado good? When the food is gone, I don't quite believe it. Like a dog, I still smell the skin. I see the oil that darkens the wood of the cutting board. Greg shrugs off his jacket and begins to unbutton his shirt. He smiles because it's Friday. I step to the sink and turn the wood over and over under the faucet, rubbing green into the grain with my fingertips. I must stop checking my phone.

The only problem is you gave me a fourth. I'm almost sure of it, and I can't imagine what kind of mess I'll find if I find it. I remember packing that morning: somewhere between rolled up jersey knits and soft denim skirts, I planted that avocado like a seed. I still see myself crouched over the suitcase, and I watch the busy hands of a dumb, rosy-cheeked girl who thought she had something special to hide, something rich promised to her.

STORY OF A ROOM

I. The Room

There's a region near the middle of the country. Cows' and goats' coats turn celadon from the potency of the grass. In this landlocked place we find a pale yellow room. It's the size of a sweet loaf—more pound than angel food—more light than dark—but not unheavy. Inside, nine objects wait to be discovered: one made of tin, one that makes noise, and one that holds all of her fear. There is softness and stillness and rough-dry paper smudged with the ink of writing performed by a left hand. And two

II. Hidden Things

other things harbored in opaque vessels. A furry creature crouches behind the carved wooden leg of a bench that's Baroque but unappreciated for its intricacy. The wood smells like dark grape skins. We appreciate that it helps hold our heroine. We don't care that it shelters the animal; the animal's importance to our story is small enough to replace the pit of an olive, but when it wets its tongue against the roof of its mouth, it sounds almost human. She does not listen. She feels

III. Her Treasure

for the charm around her neck—still warm from the oven—then the earrings (one is missing; count it as one of the objects in the room, one of two that cannot be seen unless we know how to look inside of something else, and she is learning). Last night we dreamt about her missing earring. We see it in our mind's eye. Ruby? No. Sapphire? Not emerald either. Maybe just gold or silver or something carved from the bone of an animal without fear. She unburdens

IV. Relative to Another

her ear from the remaining earring: a black pearl set in white gold above an aquamarine. Pearl and aquamarine, as though he, the jeweler, wanted us to think of the ocean, as though we, the dreamers, have been missing the ocean, and as though she, the heroine in this landlocked region in a yellow room smaller than a breadbox and no bigger than a loaf of bread, remembers how it feels to willingly merge the body into another moving body:

V. The Senses

cold and alive, salty, full of food and death, and foam and waves of death washing into food for more life. She puts the earring in her mouth and bites the swell of the pearl, rends it from the stone with a snap. Smoothing it with her tongue and teeth it tastes of concentric circles and slate. To keep it safe, she nestles it in her belly button as the animal yawns. *Where's the other?* She reads the question in the back of its webbed throat. We imagine

VI. Relative to Another

cutting through the animal's skin, muscle, and stomach to search for what she's lost (what we dreamed), but there's no knife in this room. (We would be fools to imagine a knife in this room.) The animal closes its snout and rocks on its haunches. It wobbles like an empty nesting doll. Then it is as still as the dead man who carved most of the region's well-regarded nesting dolls. In the moments that follow, it convulses and coughs,

VII. Her Treasure

quickening the flesh of its throat. Nothing precious comes up. How unfair, she thinks. We, too, bristle at the pain of the mouse and our defied expectations. To our heroine's credit, she has begun to feel the weight of her unkindness. Whether in sympathy for the rat (that used to be a mouse) or as a symptom of the pearl hunkered in her navel, she's overcome by the need to hold the animal, to inhale its carbon-based stink and feel it squirm out of her arms and hear it fall to the floor—

VIII. Hidden Things

There is no despair once you let go. Was that no fear or no despair? Was that her voice or the animal's? Is the pearl ocean-derived or fresh water? It occurs to us now that the mouse is a placeholder for a lover and the pearl for a child. It occurs to us that the lover is a placeholder for the mother and the mouse for a child. It occurs to us now that we want to be held in place as long as possible, provided the place has heat and potable water.

IX. The Room

The loaf of a room is quite pleasant. But if she tries to sleep, there will be too much light. If she tries to run, she will meet a billowing resistance. (Every creature—every object—is possessed of its own resistance.) If she tries to become a green-coated goat, she will be called a witch, so she will forget about finding the object that holds her fear; she will live alongside the tin pitcher and rusted bell, the damaged mouse and missing earing, the fancy bench and the rough-dry paper on which we've written this story.

BODIES OF WATER

I knew my mother was leaving when I heard dogs bark in the middle of the night. The neighborhood dogs were the first to know when something was wrong, and they woke me up three nights in a row before I figured it out. This was early June, a full month before the police released their warning that an entire family had been murdered. By early June we only knew about the women: the one who went missing from the mall parking lot late May, hers the body that hadn't been found, and the body that had, the other woman, a Jane Doe dredged up from the alligator pond, her flesh etched with the kind of wounds that could have made the alligators sick.

"For an alligator not to eat a body," my patchily-bearded father announced at the dinner table, the newspaper at his elbow. "That's a crime against nature." He was always talking about crimes against nature or God, though never in a religious way. My mother and I had heard it so many times we knew which words he'd stress, where his pitch would fall and rise. I'd recently overheard my mother on the telephone telling someone that my father (she didn't refer to him as her husband anymore) was a self-righteous academic who lived to hear his own voice. Maybe he was. At dinner Mom sat silently, an untouched plate of noodles in front of her, her long, thin hands resting palms up in her lap.

I wondered where my mother went at night, and I worried for her. At fourteen, I was supposed to be the one breaking out into Gainesville's summer darkness. I was supposed to have bruises on my knees and in the creases of my elbows from climbing through windows. Except I had nowhere to go. My best friend, Rachel, had been sent to a teenage-girl boot camp in Tennessee. A teacher had found her, a middle-school girl, stoned under the bleachers during a high school baseball game. The pot smoking itself wasn't such a terrible crime, but it came on the heels of so many skipped classes and my confession to her mother that she was dating Eli, an indie rocker from Athens, Georgia (she was, and they were having sex with lambskin condoms, and even—or especially—naïve virgins like me knew you couldn't count on lambskin).

Without Rachel, my mother was all I had. We watched the Home Shopping Network to marvel at the women who called. No matter the product—Santa Claus mugs, ruby rings, embroidered sheets—their on-air testimonials bloomed heavy and strange with loneliness. Almost always the women spoke of those absent from their lives: dead husbands, sisters, parents. My mother and I watched the faces of the hosts, listened to the language they used to shoo the caller off the line. Sometimes we couldn't help laughing: when a caller's passion for a spice rack intertwined with her feelings for a deceased grandmother. Or the woman who insisted that during his hospice her Harry was so comfortable propped and enveloped by the goose down duvet and pillow set. My mother joked about the comfort of Harry's morphine drip, but I didn't want to laugh because it made me feel mean. I wasn't, either, not then, not yet.

Some nights my mother stayed. Still, once I understood she was leaving—the neighborhood dogs' throats keening, vibrating my bedroom window—I wondered what kept her coming back. And I wanted to go. Since I couldn't ask, I'd hide in the station wagon, wait for her there so she'd have to take me along. I chickened out two nights in a row, but the third night, I pretended to be engrossed in one of the monochromatic art films my father had rented. My parents had gone up to their bedrooms—my father's the master and mother's the guest—so I made myself a pitcher of lemonade, sat in my father's chair, and drank the pale sugar water glass after glass, hoping I wouldn't fall asleep. I made it to midnight—my mother never left before midnight, usually not until two or three—and crept into the garage.

The car swaddled me in stuffy heat. I stripped off my blue terrycloth pants, rolling them up to use as a pillow—better against my cheek than vinyl upholstery. I curled into a fetal position in the backseat. My mother's plastic sandals peeked out from under the passenger seat. There was sand on the floor, too. We hadn't been to the beach. But that was the last I remembered of waiting for her.

It was something my father said, and though I didn't want to believe it, my mother was an appalling driver. Though I'd started on the seat, I awoke on the floor of the car. I'd hoped to wake up when my mother opened the door—when the car was still in the garage—not while we were on the road. And now my bladder stung with lemonade bloat, every bump bringing me closer to peeing. Without pants, and with the A/C streaming, I wore a suit of goosebumps.

My bladder pulsed; I envisioned the burst, then the dreamy-warm soak of pee. I clenched my leg muscles and tried to ignore the sensation verging on pain. The sand on the floor tickled: the grains jumped and skittered as we drove over uneven road. My bladder vibrated, stretched. It felt sort of sexual. Rachel had said sex when you had to pee made orgasms better. But she said she still hadn't had an orgasm, so this was irrelevant. It was the new virginity, she said, not coming. If you came you swapped souls a little, and that was major.

Rach had gone on (she liked to talk to me about sex because I was pathetically naïve), something about orgasms and trees falling in the woods with no one to hear. In her personal philosophy, it didn't make a sound. Like it never happened.

"But climaxing is loud, right?" I'd asked. Even if she hadn't managed it herself, Rach had seen porn, the close-up, shiny-slick pink stuff.

"Sure, Bea. The muscle contractions act like a megaphone in your pussy."

Who was Rachel to throw around the word pussy?

I found all of this—trees falling, souls swapping, and pussy talk—alarming. Fascinating. But thinking of it lying in the car less than three feet from my mother and not wearing pants was gross. And I had to pee bad. So bad. I clenched and kept clenching, pressing my thighs together until it felt like the bones touched.

What if my mother had a lover? What if he got into the car with her, and they proceeded to fuck there in front of me? She flipped on the interior light right then, as though she'd heard my thoughts. I had thought the word "fuck." I was a good kid. We didn't use that word in our house.

My mother rustled in her purse, but she didn't turn around. Was she eating a mint? In junior high mints foreshadowed kissing. But how could my mother be in love?

Now my eyes and bladder burned. The pain was bright.

Mommy.

Hot liquid ran down my thighs. I found a wad of drive-through napkins under the seat, and I stuffed them against the puddle forming under my left hip. I wanted to punch the seatback, but I felt pathetic and soupy. The sharp smell of my piss was rising, and soon my mother would breathe it. The raspy-loud air conditioning would circulate the stink of the baby in the back seat, and she would crash the car. Without a seatbelt, I'd be dead.

How bad was dead? Grandma was better off dead according to my mother. Dead wasn't better for those murdered women. I had thought about death before, but as a fugitive in the back seat of the car in a puddle of my own fluids, I managed startling profundity. I realized I had a choice in the matter: if I wanted, I could open the door and jump out. Depending where we were (I had no idea), and how fast we were going (fast, very fast), and the density of traffic (the road sounded lonely, but even so), I might scrape my body raw against the pavement and bleed out. Or snap my neck. Though I'd most likely just end up maimed beyond recognition.

My mother coughed a cough that sounded like "rabbit." She needed another mint. My mother probably didn't want me to die. She'd have to be a sociopath to want that. Nobody wanted their child to die first. Though my history teacher Mrs. Wagner had told me about mercy killings once after class. "Rabbit," my mother coughed again, then put a CD into the car stereo.

Joni Mitchell. Songs weren't anything like tattoos. My mother began to sing along; she sang the same note over and over, never getting anywhere. As she sang I felt a different shame. It hurt that I was in the car with her, listening to her sing badly. Joni was her favorite, and still she sang off key. The CD had more than one album on it, I think, because the music kept playing after I'd counted at least a dozen songs. I draped my pants over my legs, a makeshift blanket. I'd read that mothers could smell their babies. Even their adult offspring. Mothers could pick out their child's bed sheets from the bed sheets of dozens of children. Clammy in my puddle of pee, I wondered how my mother could drive along, singing, without any idea that her daughter shivered in the back seat.

The car slowed. If we had been on the freeway, we weren't anymore. Something—streetlight or moonlight—crept through the windows so faintly that I only noticed because a bar of it illuminated my toes. When my mother killed the engine, she waited for Joni to finish the chorus before she removed the key. We'd arrived. I popped my head up, and Mom screamed.

"God, Bea." She was rocking and breathing, her hands clasped at her chest.

I hadn't meant to pop up like that, not as nonchalantly as I had. But in my right hip was a cramp as deep as the bone. "I must be sleep-walking again, huh?"

"My heart hurts, that's how badly you scared me."

"Sorry." I held onto my pants. "I didn't mean to." She didn't buy the sleepwalking, even if I had done it a few years ago.

"You are a strange child."

I wasn't though. She was the strange one, straying into the night. I wanted to say that, but I couldn't. "Where are we?" Despite the darkness, I clearly saw we were parked at the beach; I needed to know where she thought we were.

"I couldn't sleep." She studied me. "We might as well get out of the car."

I tried to put on the pants when she wasn't looking, but she caught sight of me under the car's cracked dome light and came over to inspect the backseat.

"Is that urine?"

"The bumps jostled my bladder."

"Jostled? You talk like your father." She opened the passenger's side door, then produced a wad of napkins—always fast food napkins—from the glove compartment. "Don't put your pants on yet."

I nodded, sitting in the back with my legs hanging out of the car. My mother handed me half the napkins. With the rest, she blotted my legs. She started with my right hip, so I worked on my left ankle. I felt my shoulders slump and my child's belly stick out. I should have been more embarrassed as she touched me, but I was relieved. She wasn't there to meet anyone.

Once I was dressed and out of the car, the wind whipped my pants. My mother, seeing my bare shoulders hunched in the cold, took off her sweatshirt and handed it to me. "I forgot the blanket," she said, stepping back to the car to get it. She looked at my bare feet, then removed her own shoes and put them in the trunk. Now we were both barefoot. "You didn't have any shoes to begin with, did you?"

I shook my head.

We walked toward the ocean, then away from the light of a pier, along a stretch of beach where the sand was hard-packed and cold. Red-bellied jellyfish had washed up, so ugly they looked like bloody sanitary pads littering the shore. I was careful not to step on them, but for all my care, I cut the fleshy part of my foot on a broken shell. I kept quiet. The damp sand made it difficult to know whether or not I was bleeding.

We sat down, further from shore so we wouldn't wet the blanket. I thought about leaning against my mother's shoulder, but I didn't. I wondered how it would feel to be caught in the pull of the water—maybe something like rolling down a steep, grassy hill. I couldn't make my mother look at me, but I looked at her, her dark hair pulled back in a clip, a piece escaping to cover her left eye. Water should be clean. I wanted to wash myself in the water; wash my sliced-up foot, wash the urine off of my legs, wash the skin off of my muscle, and the muscle off of my bones. The air smelled of dead fish, though. I couldn't trust that the water was clean. I had a keen nose and knew that nearby something was dying.

"I'm unhappy, Bea."

The waves crashed against my mother's breath. I tried to match mine to hers.

"I'm leaving for now." She had found a piece of driftwood and was making cross-hatchings in the sand.

I had to say something.

"Do what you need to do, Anne," was what I said.

"Anne?"

"I don't want you to be sad," I said.

I never told my father the whole story. The story was mine. I said I was still up watching movies when Mom came downstairs, that she invited me to the beach. I didn't tell him what she had told me. She was gone a week later. She didn't make us casseroles to freeze or pack us lunches or anything like that. She left with a couple of suitcases, and we found out later that she hadn't even told her parents. A stop at the bank and she'd been on her way.

The cut on my foot got infected. I had to swallow spoonfuls of bubblegum-flavored antibiotic syrup and get stitched up once the pus stopped oozing. Seawater was supposed to work as a cleansing agent, nature's best bacteria basher, but so much for that. At least it healed in time to put on shoes for the first day of school. Rachel made it back from boot camp, too, but she couldn't keep her eyes off her cell phone. On the first day of ninth grade, she got a text from her boyfriend, Eli, saying another body had washed up, this one about 80 miles away in St. Augustine. Once she told me I shook for an hour, sure it was my mother's.

Rachel said I needed a distraction, so after school that day we met up with Eli and his friend Paul at Lake Alice. Paul's uncle was in federal prison; somehow we all knew. He'd killed a man. Or raped a kid. That's what people said. But Paul had toddler-white hair and pretty skin. He wore cologne—woody and fresh—which seemed at the time like a nice effort. Like an upstanding thing to do. Paul didn't know my mother had left me for nothing. Not for love, not for anything except to be gone. I let him touch my breasts and put his hand in my underwear. By then we knew the dead woman was only seventeen, the youngest yet. Pretty soon, Paul had shoved some fingers in me: two, maybe even three. It hurt and then it stopped hurting. And it was so sloppy I might have peed a little on his hand. But Paul didn't care; it was muggy and he smelled so good the mosquitoes wanted him. "Alright," he kept saying, "alright." He guided my hand into his jeans, and I knew: I hadn't just thought the body was hers—I'd wanted it to be.

OUR DAUGHTER

Ever wish we'd picked another? You whisper at Mary's party. Our daughter spits on her candles, dives into an ice cream cake with both fists. You bind her in a blanket while I cut cake for children too curious to eat. *And isn't that girl adopted, with the blond braid and black eyes?* I place a paper plate before her, chance recipient of Mary's blue frosting rose. Her irises wick smoke toward the ceiling, the trail twining balloon tales.

This year my fear is lighter but expanding. (I am lighter.) You said, *we should have bought a fighting fish.* (We're expanding.) I said, *I'm scared.*

Mary, our dear birthday girl, ten years ago today you split a fourteen year old open in the back of a cab. After the party you'll scream *I want my real mother* while we catch in your throat. But it's love that makes the world thick and strange, viscous and slow as the mucous-rich blood you once wore like a robe.

THE GLASS GIRL

Kella's mother waited for the orange day to fill her daughter's body, and when the bedroom was heavy with beauty, she stood, her hovering mouth so close it made fog on Kella's skin. With white cotton gloves, she stroked her daughter's smooth, hard curves. Ever the gloves, as a mother's bare hand stuck and stuttered over the surface of a girl made of glass.

Kella opened blown glass eyes. Mostly blind, and nearly deaf, she sensed vibrations keenly: when her mother hummed or stubbed a toe on the bedframe.

"Let me rub your back," her mother said. Slightly cool, Kella's body was succor to her widowed mother.

"You will polish me down to nothing," Kella said. She disliked mornings. "The walls are cracked. I feel their long lines."

"The walls are blue," her mother said. "The sky is cracked."

In truth the sky was fine. Her mother was always frightened of something. Fire, flood, or wind. That morning she'd woken from a dream about stones raining down on their house. All manner of minerals—quartz and pyrite, soft calcium, hard emerald—pocking the shingles, lodging chunks of diamond and topaz into the meat of the roof. Iron and cobalt ripped the gutters right off. Violence took a different form each night in her mother's lonely bed, and it wore out her heart.

Kella had dreamt of planets she'd never seen: cubes of rock, octahedrons of ice, and pyramids of ash (her favorite). At school they recited the planets according to separation from the sun. By distance, the teacher had said, but Kella knew the Sun preferred Mercury to Venus, Venus to Earth, Earth to Mars—

Kella pushed her mother's hand away— "You make too much static." Today, like the days before, she would ask her mother for what she wanted most: "Mother of fat and bone," Kella began, "of skin and hair and teeth and blood, may I go to school?"

Like before, her mother tried to polish the thoughts from Kella's head. She closed her lips and moved her hands.

"The faster you rub, the better I read your thoughts," Kella warned.

Her mother's face fell. Not school. The question came as a betrayal. One day it would pierce her heart through. On soft slippers, she moved to the door and locked her daughter inside.

Kella wasn't alone. Two mice, the kindly pair living behind a furnace pipe, scampered up the bedpost, settling in the concave plateau of Kella's chest.

"I didn't invite you." She brushed them to the floor, pinching the Mrs.'s tail between wrist and rib on their way down.

Kella sliced at the doorjamb with her long, glass nails.

One day, men had been Earthbound, and the next, they'd touched the Moon. It was true and irreversible; the rocket's launch, the canon's fire, the infant's crowning skull—it couldn't be undone. The disapproving eyes of the mice bore into her back. "Mice don't understand!" she hissed. Kella jabbed and slid around the lock, working for a release. She concentrated on the memory of her teacher's words traced upon her body: *Thursday* and *space shuttle*. The door opened.

Shards of fingernails had fallen to the floor, where they were retrieved by the mice—perhaps for use as mouse cutlery. Kella hadn't felt much pain wearing her beautiful nails down to their moons.

Freed from her bedroom, condensation appeared on Kella's skin. Her mother was bathing. She dashed into the master bedroom where her mother no longer slept; everything in that room remained the way it was before. Her father's comb and handkerchief on the dresser, a bottle of cologne. Kella felt inside a glass dish—a few coins, all with men's heads on them—and finally, wrapped in a soft square of fabric, Kella's glasses. She had to sit, so great was the heaving in her chest, in order to weave the thin arms through her hair. Wearing her glasses, Kella could admire the photograph of her father perched on the bedside table. Despite the thick lenses, she saw none of the details of his whiskered face, nothing but a warm, red pulse within the frame that helped her remember him.

The lenses hadn't grown foggy. Her mother must have finished the bath and would soon come to check on Kella. Kella wrapped the fuzzy blanket at the foot of the bed around herself. She dashed through the halls, the hard balls of her feet thumping against lacquered wood. Kella then opened and shut the door to her mother's world.

The path to school resembled Orion's belt; she knew the steps by heart, just as she knew the feeling of her fingertip over a raised map of constellations. The cement sidewalk etched the soles of her feet while *Thursday*, *space shuttle*, and *loneliness* danced across her skin; the looping S's tickled marvelously. *Thursday.* Thursday smelled of citrus and warm bicycle tires. *Space shuttle.* Kella would be the only child brave enough to orbit outer space. She would be able to breathe there.

The children were more surprised to see Kella than her strange beige blanket dress. The teacher smiled. The space shuttle stood in the corner of the classroom. Big as a refrigerator, its crinkled aluminum skin gleamed. Sitting several meters away at her desk, Kella drank up its blue light.

The teacher decided it was time. A small girl named Ruby led Kella to the rocket. "You have to crawl inside. Through there." Ruby pointed then pushed Kella's blanket-swathed rear to hurry her along. When Kella bumped her knee, she drew in a sharp breath. The fracture bloomed high into her hip. Nothing to fear, she told herself, it was just a fine wobbly line reaching for the sun. The door scraped against the linoleum tiles—a raspy sound that gave the children goose bumps like squeaky chalk on the blackboard—and closed. Kella waited inside the shuttle, its magic-marker smell engulfing her despite the round hole the teacher had cut away. Its close walls held mysteries the walls of her bedroom did not.

The children stared at Kella's face through the viewport—so different from theirs—the overhead halogens pooling inside her like a pitcher filling with lemonade.

"Are you ready to blast off, Miss Kella?" the teacher asked.

Kella's face remained a lighted mask—sculptural, elegant, a bit too geometric, rather like the Brancusi the students would see on their visit to the art museum. But after a moment, the glass girl nodded.

"Ten, nine," cried the chorus of children. They had not grown tired of this, not after nineteen launches in recent days, each captured by the teacher's magic camera. "Eight! Seven!"

Kella crouched in her spacecraft and remembered a story she'd heard from a different teacher. About a girl named Persephone who lived half her life underground. Kella hadn't liked that idea—she would rather be way up high than deep down low. Up high she'd be as weightless as she appeared on Earth. She would make it up to her mother by bringing her back a piece of the sky. A moon rock, perhaps. One ribboned with flecks of red and blue. Enough moon rocks to fill a candy dish! Golden butterscotches and bites of the moon for the crystal dish in the living room. Guests would marvel, their mouths watering, and her mother wouldn't have to be alone.

"Blast off, Astronaut Kella!" the children sang. The teacher snapped a picture. Kella prepared to greet the stars.

PIN: A FAIRY TALE

A designer drew up a maternity collection that premiered in the spring. The clothes bunched and bagged and made the models, long slips of ladies with volleyballs bandaged against their abdomens, appear paunchy.

How could the designer design for the pregnant woman when she'd never known the glorious swell of child?

So many people asked the question, it ruined the designer's career.

But her models still loved her.

One grew fond even of the volleyball; she kept it Ace-bandaged to her body. It bobbed with her breath when she offered to carry a child for the designer.

But she didn't quite carry it.

This model emptied her uterus into a copper pot.

The pot was not the right place for it.

She poured it into a great glass jar where she'd been culturing kombucha. After many months, a child emerged from the kombucha-soaked womb. She was no bigger than a thread of kombucha, no bigger than a pin.

The designer held her daughter, Pin, and recovered inspiration.

People began to wear the designer's slippery silks in muted colors.

Although Pin matured quickly into a lovely young lady—you should have seen her cheekbones—she remained so thin she could sleep stretched out on a needle.

Crouched in a thimble, she wouldn't leave her mother's side.

The model became jealous. She longed for the designer's love, and her uterus had pickled in the kombucha. That wasn't right. She snuck into the designer's workroom and wove Pin into a jumpsuit that was part of a collection heading for Hong Kong.

During Hong Kong fashion week, Pin was pressed against a model's hip. The model removed Pin at the midpoint of the catwalk.

Surprised, she showed the other models backstage.

Pin became their tiny mascot.

They didn't like their bodies, and Pin, being no bigger than a pin, didn't like hers either. They didn't speak the same language, but really, they did.

Mostly, the models found compassion for Pin. Even if we grow ugly, we will find other things to do with our lives, they said, but Pin will die young because technological advancements have not kept pace with the needs of her weak little heart.

On a night when they had something to celebrate, the models took Pin out with them. One of the models, older and thicker than the others, dropped Pin in a cup of kombucha.

Pin's face was so small, it generally appeared contented. The models assumed Pin was enjoying her beauty soak, but really, she drowned.

WE USED TO PLAY AT KMART

We broke the shoes apart. I gnawed through the plastic loop that joined left to right until you found the knife in the parking lot. We galloped across linoleum, our feet swimming in loafers. In red high tops we raced down the toilet paper aisle, our fists pounding the packages as we ran. In pointy-toed flats or high heels with bows, we clomped past Barbies and Legos and ugly resin horses, and we fell down—bruised our knees, elbows, chins, and thighs, deep dark fresh magic-marker purple bruises we flashed at mothers loading diapers into carts or teenage boys holding skateboards.

We didn't know he was watching.

Sometimes we snuck off to eat French fries across the street. In the store we found food other customers had opened—a box of granola bars with one already missing, a punctured bag of cheese curls. Remember when you took Excedrin from a tampered bottle because we'd heard about people poisoned and wanted to push our luck? We put Mickey Mouse stickers on each other's faces. You put stickers where I'd get boobs. Once an old woman came out of nowhere as we tore into a bag of apple candy. I said she'd turn us in, so we ran to Automotive. If we got caught, you said you'd take the blame. With green candy clenched between our teeth, we threw a steering wheel cover back and forth like a Frisbee. He saw it all. Did you know?

Together we were everything. We owned the store, which is why it didn't seem right that you never looked for me. Even if Mom told you it was supposed to happen that way, me getting snatched up in the middle of the fucking bra and underwear carousels, it wasn't right. Did you help him? Because my message from the gas station should have scared you into looking or telling the police or at least that stupid guidance counselor, Mr. Lance. I would have searched for you.

I'm seven states away now. Farther than you've ever been. I have a brown dog, Raisin, and I don't have to waste my time in a dumb discount store, but you should know I didn't want to go, and if I ever see you it won't be the same. I'm not the same. There are plenty of aunts and a grandma here, but I barely knew the man who made purple bruises around my wrists. They say I look like him. He doesn't look like you. And the shoes I walked away in—the froggy rain boots with eyes printed all wrong—weren't mine. They hurt my feet.

RECORD FROM A FARMHOUSE

We're thirsty, and Warren won't stop making snowflakes. With brittle plastic scissors, he excises wobbly circles, sickly triangles, and more quadrilaterals than the other shapes combined. Pieces of paper fall to the floor and stick to the sweaty soles of his feet; I find them in my bed, gray with dirt and a little bit translucent.

We don't light candles. The sun appears now, and it seems best to use it. Warren stands before the window that lit his great-grandmother's chair—I know from the photographs in an album my mother long ago misplaced—and it's hard to ignore the sense that the dead woman holds him there. It's her quilt that snags discarded bits of paper snow, as though it's a great net gathering us up.

"That's a good one, huh?" I ask. He's stopped showing me his scissor work. "You made it symmetrical," I add, joining my palms before opening them, hinged at the pinkies, like butterfly wings. But he doesn't look.

I haven't worked for more than a year. There's nothing to do. The bones and flesh of this house make for isolation as great as anything I can remember. Isolated but never alone; they've all lived here, all our blood has walked these floors, breathed this air. Maybe they watch, laughing to see him cutting snowflakes from yellowed paper; he's never seen snow. Then again, the difference between the snowflake in life—a bit of cold, bright hope—and his jagged imitation—it doesn't matter what he's seen.

"The wave is soft," Warren whispers into the light.

His lips are cast in shadow and his eyelids and the sweet bridge of his nose.

"They'll cover us like a blanket," he says. "Like Old Haddie's quilt."

He stares into a landscape drier and hotter than his ancestors knew, and the wave he sees still hasn't appeared to me. I think of an old book my mother read in school. An ancient book about children who must leave their parents behind to start fresh on another planet, a living planet. "Their Gods look like devils," my mother had said. And when I asked her how a devil looked, she answered: "Towering. With great veined muscles, and insect wings erupting through pulsing flesh. They have forked tails." Everything the adults in the book knew was wrong. And that the world would go on without them wasn't much consolation.

"What color is the wave today?" I ask my son.

"Raw yolk." He doesn't turn away from the light. "It has been for..." he stops, pinching his fingers together inside the holes of his snowflake, counting them, one at a time. "For seven days."

"And how far away?"

He turns to me abruptly, a frown shattering his angel-boy countenance. "You don't see it at all?" An accusation.

"My eyes," I try to explain. From years of working in the dark.

"It's over our heads." He folds his snowflake, tucks it into his pants pocket, and hands me the scissors. "It's already here."

MAN SKATE

From the outside the roller rink looked like the warehouse where my father had stocked office supplies before he left my mother and me. But inside the rink pulsed muscle and meat, sugar and syrup, a maze of what ifs like I'd never seen. It smelled of sweaty socks and licorice whips and nighttime. The air was as cool inside as out, and I was surprised by the twirling lights, the taffy and cotton candy, the quarter play Pac Man, Asteroid, and Mario Bros next to a machine dispensing a rubber ball for a nickel.

The colored lights of the rink reminded me of the rock we'd cracked open in Mrs. Rothby's science class. She never said there would be another world inside, so when she unscrewed the vise, I fell in love with her and the network of crystals she held up to her chest. A geode over Mrs. Rothby's heart, the flickering of deep purple jewels: I wanted her to take me home and tuck me into bed with the sheets pulled up to my chin.

But it was Uncle Roy who held my hand at the skate rental counter. I had a fresh scrape on my left palm from a skateboarding fall, so I turned and gave him my right. It was the two of us, Roy taking me on my first trip to the roller rink. I remember getting boy's skates because I had a wide foot. Uncle Roy brought his own skates: black boots with neon wheels. My rentals, size four, were a dirty naugahyde—not quite vinyl, not quite animal—with pumpkin orange wheels. Chocolate brown laces. I looked at Uncle Roy squatting in his tight acid jeans, lacing me up as I sat on a large, carpeted stool shaped like a mushroom. These mushrooms were everywhere, along with more kids than I'd ever seen: bigger kids, better kids, kids flashing glittered wrist bands and heavy metal t-shirts. The boys, I watched the boys pull off their high tops, shed sweatshirts to reveal tanks and flesh—biceps, triceps—I wanted to touch the skin over those muscles. I wanted it to be silly putty so I could leave fingerprints.

The rink played the same song we'd heard in Uncle Roy's car. Poison, they were his favorite band. Uncle Roy had freckles along his temples and forehead that never made it to his nose. He began to lace me up even though I asked to do it myself. I saw my father a couple times a year then, and he let me do everything myself. But Uncle Roy insisted helping me into the skates, his cupped palm against my arch, then his fingers running up my heel like a shoehorn. He had dry lips. He'd laced me up too tight and had to wrap the extra length around my ankle before tying them in one bow, then another. The skates pressed on the round bone on the inside of my ankles.

"You're ready, Erin." He grinned up at me like I was the most fabulous person he'd ever seen. "You're gonna blaze a trail."

He got up to sit next to me. I had to watch him put on his own skates, and I think he took a extra time fooling with eyelets, re-lacing, because he liked feeling my eyes on him.

Roy was my mother's younger brother. He was a secretary at the dairy plant. The first time we were truly alone together (my mother busy taking her final nursing exam), he'd brought me to the plant's "dairy museum," where I saw the evolution of pasteurization equipment and photographs of a life-sized Holstein sculpted in butter. At the end of the tour I drank a pint of chocolate milk; Roy tipped the corner of his into mine. "Cheers," he'd said.

Uncle Roy and Grandma had encouraged my mother to attend nursing school after my father left. Mom got a job at a nursing home while she worked toward her degree. After school I'd take the city bus to the home to watch television with the residents who liked westerns and *I Love Lucy*. I could barely see the TV because a blind, retarded woman sat right in front of it. The old people felt sorry for her—she still had creamy-smooth skin—so they let her press her palms to the screen.

Government cuts took my mother's job at the home, so she settled for the night shift at a hospital. I stayed at Grandma's, then with Uncle Roy. My mother tried to make it so we had dinner together. We ate from a can, but she always heated it on the stove. I loved her, and I knew she was good because one day I asked her about the commercials with the starving black kids and their huge stomachs. Give seventy-two cents a day, the TV said. Less than the cost of one cup of coffee. My mother told me those kids' bellies weren't fat. Bad bacteria produced gas that blew up their stomachs like balloons. She said it was very painful; one day when we had a little money she would call the number. I'd already asked Uncle Roy that same question. He didn't know why starving kids were fat, just that the flies on their faces made him want to puke.

"Don't be afraid to grab me if you lose your balance," Uncle Roy said. I wasn't afraid, and I wouldn't fall. In gym class, I was the best: the first girl picked for teams and second-best of all the fourth graders for chin ups—seventeen. We stood at the edge of the rink, where carpet met wood, waiting for an opening in the stream of skaters. A breeze found my face as people whooshed by. That air smelled different, a little like fruit punch. Boys held girls' hands.

"Should we do it?" he asked.

We stepped onto the rink. He grabbed at my hand but missed and held my fingers. I didn't want to look like a baby. There were some other kids with dads holding their hands, but they looked like toddlers in glorified Fischer Price skates. That wasn't me.

I pulled my hand away.

Uncle Roy grabbed for it again, but I kept it out of reach until he gave up.

Roller skating wasn't any harder than skateboarding. I had the neighbor kid's old Santa Cruz and sometimes rode it down Grandma's driveway. She told me I'd break my neck. I loved her, but she was all cigarette smoke and hype. She promised to crack my head open if I didn't wear the jumpers my mother sewed me. There wasn't anything better than the couple times a year I saw my dad because he pulled the dresses out of my overnight bag and laughed at them. Flowers? Rosebuds? We'd make gagging noises together, then go to the hardware store to buy screws and drill-bits.

There was a DJ booth built into the far wall. Inside a man wearing a camouflage jacket spoke into a microphone. He said things like: "Here's a song for city folk," and "If you know how to live it up on Friday night, this is for you." He didn't annoy me, but I kept thinking that if I had a microphone, I'd say something that mattered: why the starving kids' stomachs looked fat or that it's stupid to make people wear dresses.

I was skating better—I even managed to vary my speed—but Roy stayed next to me. He probably didn't have many friends if he'd volunteered to baby-sit. He wasn't cool, so I pretended he wasn't right there, smelling a little like onions. I thought about who I'd like to be skating with, whose hand I would want to hold. Mrs. Rothby's.

But she wore fancy shoes with heels, and I couldn't imagine her in skates. I surveyed the skaters around me, eventually spotting a cute girl. She looked about thirteen and wore a ponytail with a pink ribbon. Girls needed pretty things. Colored spots of light revolved around the rink, blurring the walls blue, red, and green. They stained the skaters too. My girl turned purple—her blouse and skin—then yellow, orange. I skated just behind her. Her boyfriend wore a baseball cap for Detroit. I had that hat. But Grandma didn't like me to wear it.

When the DJ announced the Man Skate, I felt a crawling in my stomach. To think of it now, it was like those seconds when you're scratching a lottery ticket—when the first two boxes show ten thousand dollars, and you only have to match a third. It's that rush of excitement that sours as soon as the third box gets scratched.

What was a Man Skate? It sounded reptilian. Even though the composition of the rink was changing—it looked like just the girls were getting off—I stayed my course, kept skating.

"Wait over there." Roy shoved me toward the mushrooms. "You can't skate."

I wasn't stupid, but I wanted to know why. I tied for second most chin-ups. At recess I raced with the boys. "I'm better than him." I pointed at a skinny kid on the rink waving to someone by the mushrooms.

"Here," Uncle Roy wormed his hand into his jeans' pocket. "Buy some candy." He gave me a wad of paper money.

Since my allowance came in quarters, the dollars distracted me. I cupped the bills and went to the mushrooms to count the money. Most of the mushrooms were full by now. Girls. They giggled together and grabbed each other's hands. I stood at the edge of a forest, the smells and sounds thick and unfamiliar. They weren't paying attention to me, but I felt as conspicuous as the buzzing neon over the snack bar.

The men still hadn't started to skate; the sound system had malfunctioned, and the camouflage guy messed with it. I found a partially open mushroom with a view of the rink. I didn't notice at first, but my girl sat opposite, legs crossed. A head taller than me, she had her hand in her ponytail, was brushing it with her fingers. She wasn't as pretty from the front; her mouth was crooked and hungry, like my old goldfish, Bob. But her eyes were nice. I couldn't tell the color because she sort of squinted, like she really wanted to see stuff. I opened my hand to count the money. It had seemed like more, but the bills were crunchy and mangled, bulkier that way: three dollars.

Still, the roller rink was mine with three dollars: sixty bouncy balls, twelve arcade game credits, and cotton candy or pop wouldn't cost more than a dollar: three pops. I was about to walk to the snack counter when I noticed my girl looking at me. I wore brown corduroy pants—I didn't complain about those—but my shirt had a white doily bit at the collar. She looked at me like she didn't know why I had a doily around my neck. I didn't know, except that if I tried to rip it out, Grandma would rant about cracking my head.

I thought to shrug at my girl to show her I was cool, but the music for the Man Skate began. She turned to watch the rink. My eyes followed. I found Uncle Roy in the mass of skaters; he looked like a Poindexter—too tall and thin to be any good at skating.

Uncle Roy skated near the front of the pack like it was a race. My girl's boyfriend strained to keep up. Red and blue lights spun like police warnings. The bills in my hand dampened with sweat. I wanted my chin-length hair to blow back; I wanted to pump my arms and cross my legs one over another around the rink's curves; I wanted my veins to stand out from my forearms and neck like they did on my dad when he worked on the roof. My girl would see me and wonder how I could skate so fast without falling. I would wave and keep my balance. I'd even describe the Man Skate to Dad: the speed and lights, the loudest music I'd ever heard. I would tell him I was out there skating, the fastest of all.

It lasted for a couple songs, enough time for the dads to impress their kids and the boys to impress their girls. I clenched my jaw the whole time.

"Last time I was here a guy broke his arm." My heart raced at the surprise—my girl had spoken to me! Now I saw she had braces, and they made her mouth hungrier even though they made it full.

"Really?" I said, scratching my chin like Dad did.

"Yeah, I'd never want to go out there." She shook her head as she got up; her ponytail swayed.

"I would," I said.

She stopped. She hadn't expected me to say anything. She'd started the conversation out of boredom, and I told her I wanted to Man Skate. She stood there looking down at me. Her eyes really looked, squinted like she was figuring something out. Then she smiled with her lips together. A smile that closed off her face. It seemed like it would be hard to smile like that with so much metal on your teeth.

She returned to the rink, but I stayed on the mushroom. She'd peeled something away from me. And though I hadn't begun to understand what I'd lost, I knew to be thankful for the darkness and noise of the rink, for its thick, musty smell; I hoped it would hide me if I kept still.

When Uncle Roy found me at the mushroom, he was breathing hard. Sweat held his t-shirt to his skin and soaked the hair at the nape of his neck. He asked if I'd spent the money. I lied. I thought about what I could do with those three dollars. Last time I visited my dad he had his eye on a circular saw. But that was too expensive.

I didn't want to skate anymore, but Roy pulled me back to the rink. We slipped into the flow though I hardly moved my legs. Sometimes I stopped skating completely, let him drag me around the corners. As Roy's hands began to sweat, the salt made the scrape on my palm sting.

The DJ announced a song for "People who like to dance," even one for "People who have dreams." I thought I saw my girl playing Pac Man in the distance, but by the time Roy wanted to leave, she wasn't there.

I sat on the mushroom; Uncle Roy crouched below. He was trying to get my skate off, but I didn't want him to. He struggled, determined to do it even though he hadn't properly loosened the laces. My foot was wedged inside. The more he pulled, I pushed. Then, I thought I saw my girl watching; adrenalin pumped through me. Roy swore now: Jesus and shit. His fair skin pulsed a sick pink. He let go. Without his resistance, my leg swung through his face.

The toe of my skate bashed his nose, and the wheels rolled over his eyes. I felt it through my whole body. He brought his hand to his face; blood flowed. "I can do it myself," I said. And I did, while he went to the snack bar to get napkins.

No one seemed to notice what had happened. I looked for my girl. Had she witnessed my glory? As I unlaced my other skate, I squinted to see her. She was gone.

Uncle Roy returned, the napkins a bloody blossom under his nose. He glared at me as we returned my skates. My skates with the pumpkin wheels and chocolate brown laces. Just walking through the parking lot I felt like I was still rolling; my legs were not my legs anymore. It was time to get into his car again, his smelly Buick, clunky as a battleship, with cigarette burns on the dash. Uncle Roy leaned over to fasten my seatbelt, then tugged to make sure it was taut. The car soon filled with his sweaty onion smell. He turned on the radio, but I didn't know the song.

About the Author

Wendy's stories appear or are forthcoming in *Cimarron Review*, *Carve*, *Cherry Tree*, *Quarterly West*, and elsewhere. In 2015 she won the *storySouth* Million Writers Award and was a fiction fellow at the Vermont Studio Center. Based in Pullman, WA, and Los Angeles, CA, she teaches for the Writers' Program at UCLA Extension, provides creative and academic editorial services, and dabbles in true crime TV writing. She is, of course, working on a novel.

CPSIA information can be obtained
at www.ICGtesting.com
Printed in the USA
LVOW10s0925070118
562111LV00010B/255/P